Clifford's
Birthday Party

Norman Bridwell

SCHOLASTIC INC.

For Adam, James, and Patrick

ISBN 978-0-545-47956-1

10 9 8 7 6 5 4 3 2   12 13 14 15 16/0

Printed in the U.S.A.   132
This edition printing, January 2013

My name is Emily Elizabeth,
and this is my dog, Clifford.
Last week was Clifford's birthday.
We invited his pals to a party.

Mom had ice cream and cookies.
We put up decorations.

When it was time for the party to begin,
nobody was there.
Where could they be?

We went looking for Clifford's pals.

They were all together at the playground.

I asked them why they hadn't come to the party.

Jenny said they wanted to come,
but they didn't have very good presents for Clifford —
not good enough for such a special friend.

I told them not to be silly.

Clifford would like whatever they got for him.

They all ran home to get their gifts...

and everyone came to the party.

First we opened the gift from Scott and his dog, Susie.

Scott had blown it up as much as he could.

Clifford blew it up some more.

We really had a ball.

Then Clifford pulled out the stopper.

That was a mistake.

The next gift was from Sam and his dog, Lenny.
It was a piñata!

We hung the piñata from a tree.

There were treats inside for all the dogs.

Clifford was supposed to break the piñata
with a stick.
He gave a couple of good swings...

and the piñata broke open.
The dogs liked the treats...

but we decided not to give Clifford any more piñatas.

We all laughed when we saw the gift from
Jenny and her dog, Flip.
It was a little small for Clifford.

But it was just right for his nose.
Clifford hates having a cold nose.

Alisha and Nero's gift was a toy dog that talked.

Clifford thought it was cute.
He went to pet it.

Uh-oh.
They don't make toys the way they used to.

It was time for ice cream when Cynthia
and her dog, Basker, arrived.

They brought Clifford a gift certificate
from the Bow Wow Beauty Parlor.
He could get a free shampoo and haircut.

We each had our own idea of how Clifford might look after the beauty parlor.

I like Clifford just the way he is.
I thanked Cynthia for the gift,
but I slipped the certificate to Scott
and Susie. I knew she would like it.

Then came the cake. Clifford was surprised.

He was even more surprised...

when his family popped out!

He hadn't seen his mother and father
and sisters and brother for a long time.

Clifford liked the presents his friends gave him,
but having his family and friends with him
was the best birthday present of all.